Filomena's Seasons

Book Three of "The Adventures of Filomena" Series

Fernando M. Reimers

I thank the following friends for their suggestions to a draft of this story

Eleonora Villegas-Reimers, Karina Baum, Mariali Cardenas, Armando, Juan Pablo, Maria Isabel Estrada,

Vidur Chopra, John and Linda Collins, Allan Countinho, Armand Doucet, Maria Paz Ferreres,

Sofia and Tomas Marcilese, Cecilia Galas, Luis Enrique Garcia de Brigard, Cynthia Hobbs, Armida Lizarraga,

Isabel Londono, Nell O'Donnell, Vikas Pota, Juliet Baum-Snow and Catherine Snow, and David Weinstein.

Illustrations: Tanya Yastrebova

Book Layout by Tanya Yastrebova

Library of Congress Control Number: 2018914300

Kindle Direct Publishing, Seattle, Washington

To my parents, who shaped the seasons of my life

SEASONS

I love my seasons in New England. They mark life's moments. The happy and sunny long warm days of the summer. The beautiful fall when the leaves of our trees turn red and orange and yellow. The short cold days in the winter when the snow piles up on the rooftops of the houses, the branches of the trees and the sides of the streets. And finally, the spring of a thousand births, when new plants, animals and birds are born, reminding us of the hope that is each new life. They are special our seasons. Each one is unique and

different from the others. Together they take us from year to year, as we go through life.

My name is Filomena. I am a twelve-year-old parakeet. I live on School Street in a small town near the city of Boston. On weekends during the summer, Fernando takes me outside to the garden. I like spending time there. I talk with my friends and look at the many different flowers and trees. A bird feeder hangs from a lamppost and many different wild birds come to eat there. I watch three baby squirrels grab the seeds that have fallen under the birdfeeder. Liberty, the blue jay, tells them they can have as much food as they want, but they should save some for the other animals who live in the garden, because we are all connected, and we must take care of  each other. As the summer comes to an end and the air gets cooler, I watch the leaves changing colors, some of them falling and the days shortening. This is a sign that fall is coming.

As I look at the pine tree behind the lamp post I reflect. Every summer the pine tree is a little taller. Fernando planted it in that corner of the garden about ten years ago. Back then, the pine tree was only a few inches tall, barely a little taller than me. The pine tree now grows in the same spot where a beautiful big old cherry tree used to be. Each spring pink flowers blossomed on its branches. One winter day a branch fell, then another. Little by little the flowers and leaves stopped growing on its branches. One day a very big branch fell off, as if all life had abandoned the tree. That spring some gardeners came and took the old cherry tree away. It had seen many seasons in our garden. The gardeners said it had probably been planted when the house was built, one hundred years ago! When the gardeners took what was left of the lifeless cherry tree, they left an empty corner in the garden. It was there that Fernando planted the little sapling that summer.

As I watched the cherry tree grow old, it helped me understand that there are different kinds of seasons. There are the four seasons of the year that I love so much: the summer, fall, winter and spring. And there are also seasons of life for every

living creature: birds, animals, plants and people too. The three little squirrels that play in front of the pine tree are just babies, but they will grow into adults. One day maybe they will have babies. And one day they will notice they have grown old, just like the old cherry tree. Most of what they see in the garden has been here before they arrived.

Much will remain when they are gone. They are just one moment in a much longer and older tree of life, older than any of us.

The fall will be here soon. It always follows the summer. Thinking about the arrival of the fall reminds me of Winter. Not the season which follows the fall, but my friend named Winter. He was a parakeet too.

LIFE IN THE PET STORE

Winter and I arrived together in the house on School Street on the same day, eleven years ago. We had been living in a large cage in the pet store with several other parakeets, all hoping a family would adopt us and take us to their home. The pet store also had other birds and animals, and it sold food and supplies and toys for parakeets, fish, dogs and cats. Many people came to the store to look at the birds and animals and to buy things for their pets. Others brought their dogs and their cats to have their hair cut.

One day I heard a lot of noise, and saw a large group of children come in to the store with their teacher. They were taking a field trip. One boy came over to our cage and looked at me with big wide eyes. He was taller than the others, and he watched me as I jumped from one perch to another. He began to talk to me, "How are you little bird? What is your name? Do you want to be my friend?" When the school visit finished, the boy stayed behind. He didn't want to leave. His teacher called him, "Come on, Pablo. We have to go back to school."As Pablo was leaving, he turned around and whispered "I will come back. I want to be your friend." That evening, when the owner closed the store and turned off the lights, I wondered where Pablo was. Would he still be thinking of me?

MEETING THE FAMILY

A few days later, I saw a child coming right towards me. It was Pablo! He was with another boy bursting with excitement as he approached my cage. Standing behind them a man and a woman watched. Pablo pointed at me and then talked to the other boy and to the grown-ups. I was so excited! I thought I had made an impression when he first met me! The store owner approached with a small cardboard box and grabbed me and put me inside the box. There were small holes in the box. I saw the owner put another parakeet in another box. Pablo took my box and peeked through the holes to look at me. He said, "Hello parakeet. We are going to take you home. You are going to be part of our family."

We drove a short distance in a car. I looked through the holes in my box as Pablo carried

me. He got out of the car and walked up some steps into the house. Then we entered a large room and he placed my box on a table in the middle of the room. The other boy placed the other box next to mine, and I could hear my friend chirping. The man placed a large cage on the table, and the woman carried a large bag with bird seeds. Then they carefully moved us out of the boxes into the large cage. Pablo spoke excitedly, "Hi parakeet. My name is Pablo, and this is my brother Tomas. This is my mom Eleonora, and my dad Fernando, and this is your new home." Eleonora asked Pablo, "And what name are you going to give your parakeet? I think she is a female?" "Her name will be Summer," said Pablo pointing at me. Then Eleonora asked Tomas, "And how about you, Tomas? What will you name your parakeet? He is a male." Tomas said, "If Pablo's parakeet is going to be named Summer, then I will name mine Winter."

"Summer and Winter?" said Eleonora "Those are nice names." Fernando then said "The names are nice, but many people have two names. Can I give each of them a middle name? Summer looks like a Filomena to me, so let's name her Summer Filomena. And Winter looks like an Apollo to me, so let's call him Winter Apollo." Pablo replied, "Okay dad. Tomas and I will call them Summer and Winter, and you can call them Filomena and Apollo if you like." And this is how I arrived at the house on School Street on a beautiful spring day eleven years ago.

LIFE ON SCHOOL STREET

Winter and I became very good friends. We enjoyed playing with Pablo and Tomas. Every day after school, they came to play with us. One day they let us go outside the cage. They closed the doors of the living room and we flew from one end of the room to the other. When they tried to catch us, we flew away, flitting from one sofa to the next. Finally, Pablo grabbed me gently, making a

small cup with his hands, and Tomas caught Winter, to take us back to the cage.

Pablo and Tomas would change the water and put seeds in our feeder every morning. Two small doors led to the two feeders on the floor. One day, as Winter was having breakfast and I was exercising on my swing, Winter called to me excitedly, "Hey Summer, look! The door behind the feeder is open. The boys must have forgotten to lock it." The house was quiet. Pablo and Tomas were at school, and Eleonora and Fernando had gone to work. Winter got on top of the feeder, peeked outside the

door, and jumped outside, flying into the living room! I hesitated but finally decided to follow Winter too. Soon we were exploring the house. We took our time to visit every room. We danced on the keys of the piano, making musing as we jumped from one key to the next. We checked the boys' bedrooms and the books in their bookcases. We raced in the wooden toy cars Tomas and Pablo had built. We saw the bathrooms and the kitchen. We made soap bubbles with the dishwashing liquid next to the kitchen sink. It took us a long time to explore the house. At the end of the day we returned to the living room. But instead of going back to our cage, we, exhausted, decided to nap behind a sofa. The back door opening woke us up from our nap. We heard the family talking as they usually did when they returned from school and work. Tomas raced to the living room, looking for us. He stopped in shock. "Pablo, come here! You won't believe what happened." Pablo came running, "What," as he put is backpack on the floor: "What happened Tomas?" "Look!" cried Tomas: "The birds have left their

cage!" In shock Pablo called out "Mom, Dad, come here! Winter and Summer are gone!" Tomas said, "Okay, let's organize a search party. They have to be inside the house somewhere. The windows have screens, and the doors were closed, so they can't have left the house." The four of them began to look for us, calling out "Wiiiiinter, where are you?" "Helloooo, Summer. Do you want to come and play?" Winter and I looked at each other, not knowing what to do. We were having fun playing hide and seek with the family, but we didn't want them to worry too much. Finally I chirped to give them a hint. Pablo yelled, "Hey, everyone, I heard something. I think they are here in the living room." Winter

then chirped with his beautiful voice, and soon Tomas and Pablo found us. I could tell they were relieved, and happy to be able to play with us again. Of the many years we spent with Tomas and Pablo, summer was always my favorite season. It was then they had more time to play with us, and would make toys for us and change our swings from time to time. As Tomas and Pablo grew older, they got busier with school and sports. While they still came to talk to us, they didn't play with us the way they used to.

Then Tomas went to college, and two years later Pablo left for college as well. Even though I would no longer see them as often, I knew the times we had spent together had helped the boys turn into the kind young men that they were. They had learned to speak softly and to be gentle from playing with us, they had become good observers of others from watching us play, they had become good listeners, from paying attention to our chirps and trying to decipher what we were trying to say. They had learned from trying to see the world through our eyes as they spent time with us. It was as if a little of Winter and of me had gone to college with Pablo and Tomas. Winter and I had also kept a little of Tomas and Pablo in ourselves from trying to see the world through their eyes. Back in the house on School Street, there were now just four of us.

WINTER

That fall Winter my friend got sick. I began to notice that he was not feeling well when he began to sing less. Winter was always very talkative. He would be the first to greet me in the morning, and he loved to talk all day. All of a sudden, he became unusually quiet. I asked him, "What's the matter, Winter? Are you okay?" He didn't answer. I then realized he was not eating. I told him he had to eat or he would get sick. "I'm just feeling weak, Summer. I am not sure I have the strength to stand on the perch anymore." "Don't be silly, Winter. Of course you can stand on your perch." I would stand next to him, so he would lean against me. I brought him a seed or two and fed them to him. Winter would lean against me to hold himself up.

It was then that Fernando began to take the cage each day to the kitchen table in the mornings, because there was more sunlight in the kitchen and also so he and Eleonora would talk to us while they were in the kitchen. One day, when Eleonora and Fernando returned from work, they noticed something wrong. Winter was on the floor, his eyes closed. I was on my perch in silence. I had tried to wake Winter up all day, but he wouldn't move.

"Winter lived for eleven years," said Fernando as he lifted Winter out and took him outside. "That's a long time for a parakeet to live." But Winter did not move. "I will bury him next to the young little pine tree" he said. That was the last time I saw

Winter. Ever since that day, the fall makes me a little sad. But seeing the pine tree grow reminds me of my friend Winter and of the many good times we shared in the house on School Street. Those ten years we spent together, the games we played, the songs we sang, our adventures, became a part of who I am. I feel as if a little bit of Winter is with me every day, even though I cannot see him.

Looking at the pine tree, and knowing it is growing where the old cherry tree lived for one hundred years, makes me think we are all growing where others grew before us. We are moments of life connected to each other, including those who are no longer with us. My life, and the lives of Tomas and Pablo, were shaped by the years we spent with Winter, even if he is no longer with us. I may not see Tomas and Pablo as often as I used to, but I know all the time they spent with me has become a part of who they are

today and a part of who I am. And when the winter comes, with its white cold silence, I will remember how we are all part of a much bigger universe, of which each of our lives is only a brief moment, but that together all these moments make up eternity.

And as the spring arrives, as it does always, with a thousand new lives, I will enjoy every moment I can share with all life around me, in all of its wonder, knowing that this is how we leave part of ourselves in the world.

I love my seasons in New England. They remind me that time goes by, and that a life is made of moments. As with the seasons in New England, those moments can go by pretty quickly. And when we leave, the great world continues to spin. Knowing this is a reason to live our lives to the fullest. To make the most of the seasons of our lives.

QUESTIONS FOR DISCUSSION

Why does Filomena like the seasons?

What makes each season unique?

How did Filomena meet Pablo?

How did Filomena arrive in the house on School Street?

Who did Filomena arrive on School street with?

What names did Pablo and Tomas give the two birds when they brought them from the store?

What names did Pablo and Tomas' father give the birds?

What happened when winter found that the boys had left the door of the cage open?

What did Filomena discover when she walked on the keys of the piano?

What does Filomena think about when she sees the pine tree growing in the corner of the garden?

What does Filomena mean when she says there are seasons of life for every living creature?

What did Tomas and Pablo learn from playing with Winter and Filomena for so many years?

Can you think of a friend you have spent much time with? What have you learned from that friend?

Do you think you will remember that friend if one of you moves and you no longer see each other regularly?

Are there ways in which the time you spent with your parents, and the things you do together, became a part of who you are?

How do those things you do together become a part of who your parents are?

One day you may no longer live in the same house with your parents. Do you think you will remember the years you lived together?

Do you think your parents will remember those years when you lived with them?

What do you think Filomena meant when she said that our lives are just a moment in a much bigger universe?

What does Filomena mean by "knowing that life is but a moment is a reason to live our lives to the fullest?"

The Adventures of Filomena A series of books to promote intergenerational conversations about values to sustain a world that includes all, available in multiple languages as paperback, kindle and audiobooks

https://theadventuresoffilomena.squarespace.com/

In The Story of Filomena, the first book in the series, Filomena discovers that we all see the world through a frame of mind and that observation is a powerful tool to help us understand how others see the world.

In Filomena"s Friends, the second book in the series, Filomena spends many days in the garden during the summer with a diverse group of friends who enrich her life. They discover together how much friends, working together, can achieve.

In Filomena"s Seasons, the third book in the series, as the summer winds down, Filomena reflects on the passage of 29 the seasons, and realizes how they punctuate our lives. As she remembers her friend Winter, she discovers that as we spend time with others we become a part of who they are, and they become a part of who we are.

Made in the USA
Middletown, DE
15 February 2019